SYdNEY'S VACATION

Written by Loree Cowling ~ Inspired by Sydney Cowling
Illustrated by Karon Argue

Dedication

Sydney, Karon and I have truly experienced the most magnificent aspects
of life while finding our way through the most challenging of circumstances.
The gift of us all coming together to create this book so we can shine light on
the 'magic' that exists in all things is a beautiful divinely guided blessing.
Every moment on our individual journeys we have known the love, care and
deep compassion of our families and friends. We have only had to reach out a
hand to feel their support. We dedicate this book to them and to
the love that they ignite in our hearts everyday.

One day Mom said, "We are going on a vacation!"
"What's a vacation?" I asked. "What if it's scary?"
"It's an adventure where you see new places, meet new people, and try different things."

"We are going to fly on an airplane to visit the princesses at their home in Disneyland," Mom said.
I started to feel excitement and happiness inside at the idea of seeing

4

the princesses, but I was still scared about trying the new things. "Mom, I don't know how to fly. I like being at home with my own things. Do we have to go?" I pleaded.

Mom exclaimed, "I have an idea!"
She made me a magical story book about our adventure that we read
every night before I went to sleep.

6

I learned about the airplane, how to be happy instead of scared, and how much fun adventures can be.
The day of our adventure happened just like the story book.

We picked out my special toys and books to go into my very own suitcase. I was glad to know that my most favourite things would be with me.

8

They help me feel calm and happy when I'm trying new things and meeting different people.

We rode to the airport in a magical car called a taxi. It was exciting to sit in the back with my mom with our very own driver to take us to the airport.

There were special people that helped us with our suitcases.
Everyone was very friendly and kind to me and my mom.

At the airport, a lady at the counter gave us our tickets.
She had a beautiful smile and showed us where to go next.

12

There was a lineup, so Mom and I told each other jokes and laughed

I watched my backpack go into the machine that would take pictures of my special things. I loved that my precious toys had a fun adventure all their own.

"Mom, it's the magic door. Just like in our story!" I cheered.
A wonderful spell was cast as I went through the door.
I stopped thinking about my room, my friends, my grandma, and
everything back home.

"Sydney, look, it's a beautiful fairy with a magic wand," whispered Mom.

The fairy waved the wand all around me, and it filled me with excitement and happiness. I started to feel that everything to come would be full of joy.

We gathered our things and began to walk through a mystical land.

There were shops filled with special gifts, books, and strange little pillows that Mommy said are special just for the plane.

Waiting to get on the plane, I noticed that not everyone was filled with excitement and joy.

"Mommy, why are some people sad and angry, and some others seem so far away that they don't even notice us?"

"Oh my, what a wonderful question!" replied Mom.
"You see, Sydney, everyone gets to decide how they are going to have their adventure. Sometimes people can't stop thinking about all the things that are back before the magic door.

Sometimes they are stuck in their worry about what they need to do after they arrive where they are going."

"I like to be on our adventure this way, filled with excitement and joy. Letting my thoughts be here with you right now is the best way for me to do that!" explained Mom.

Just then a beautiful lady called us up to the gateway and asked if we were ready to fly away to a new magical land.
We both exclaimed, "YES!"

The door opened to a mystical tunnel. The roof was covered in twinkling starlight, and the floor glowed with glitter. We skipped and danced all the way to the entrance of the airplane.

A man in a special uniform took us to our seats and helped us get
comfortable before all the other travelers joined us.

Once the plane began to move, I felt a shaking and heard a rumbling noise.

Mom happily told me, "The plane is being filled with magic fairy dust that will carry us to our destination."

The plane lifted off the ground, and I felt a warm feeling in my heart. I was glowing with joy from the inside out. "We are flying, we are flying! I'm Peter Pan!" I shouted with glee.

I excitedly said to my mom, "Look at all these people playing the
adventure game just like us.

When the plane landed we went through another magical land that had moving sidewalks. It was so much fun to walk fast on them and feel the wind in my hair.

We came to a place where a beautiful carousel delivered our suitcases to us. Lots of happy people smiled and waved at me.

Outside the doors a carriage was waiting to take us to the home
of all the princesses. I was so excited to ride in the carriage. It
was the only thing I could think about, and my heart grew even

more filled with joy! Mom and I giggled and cuddled all the way to our destination.

"Thank you, Mommy, for taking me on a vacation! Now I know anywhere we go can be a magical adventure just like this one!"

Loree is the mother of a beautiful young woman who has chosen to shine her light as a soul with Down Syndrome. She is an author, speaker, intuitive way finder and a sacred storyteller. Loree uncovers the understandings of peoples experiences through stories, intuitive healing sessions, meditations, workshops and everyday conversations to reveal the sacred gifts that allow one to live authentically.

Sydney sees the world from a unique perspective that allows everyone she meets the opportunity to see themselves as 'perfect just the way they are'. At the age of 3 she underwent intensive treatment for Leukaemia. Due to the days and months of isolation required she spent hours watching and memorizing musicals and movies of magic that sparked her love of being on stage. Her powerful messages of acceptance, kindness and seeing through the eyes of love, deeply impact audiences.

Together they raise awareness and cultivate new understandings of inclusion consciousness projects, events and speaking engagements.

Author/illustrator Karon Argue studied art at Medicine Hat College in Alberta. She began creating fun, quirky characters when her three children were young and drew inspiration from their antics.

In 2010 Karon became legally blind. In 2015 with the help of visual aids, she wrote and illustrated, The Smooch. Karon still hand draws and colors her illustrations with pencil crayons and ink. To find out more about Karon and her journey visit www.karonargue.com

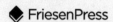

FriesenPress

Suite 300 - 990 Fort St
Victoria, BC, V8V 3K2
Canada

www.friesenpress.com

ISBN
978-1-5255-1692-4 (Hardcover)
978-1-5255-1693-1 (Paperback)
978-1-5255-1694-8 (eBook)

1. JUVENILE FICTION

Distributed to the trade by The Ingram Book Company

CPSIA information can be obtained
at www.ICGtesting.com
Printed in the USA
LVHW072050300719
625894LV00001B/2/P

* 9 7 8 1 5 2 5 5 1 6 9 2 4 *